BATMAN: YEAR ONE™

FRANK MILLER WRITER
DAVID MAZZUCCHELLI ILLUSTRATOR
RICHMOND LEWIS COLORIST
TODD KLEIN LETTERER

Adapted from the works of
Bob Kane, Bill Finger
and Jerry Robinson

Batman created by Bob Kane

TITAN BOOKS
LONDON

INTRODUCTION

If your only memory of Batman is that of Adam West and Burt Ward exchanging camped-out quips while clobbering slumming guest stars Vincent Price and Cesar Romero, I hope this book will come as a surprise.

For me, Batman was never funny. I was eight years old when I picked up an 80-page annual from the shelf of a local supermarket. The artwork on one story looked good and scary.

Gotham City was cold shafts of concrete lit by cold moonlight, windswept and bottomless, fading to a cloud bank of city lights, a wet, white mist, miles below me. The street sounds were a soft, sad roar, unbroken and unchanging.

Then somewhere, somewhere in the stone rat's maze down there, tiny but unmuffled, a pane-glass window shattered. The sound was almost pretty, like chimes. The chimes became a single ringing bell, a burglar alarm, the old kind.

A Thompson machine gun spat at the bell. A madman laughed wildly, maliciously. The laughter echoed forever.

A shadow fell across me, from above. Wings flapped, close by and almost silent.

Glistening wet, black against the blackened sky, a monster, a giant, winged gargoyle, hunched forward, pausing at a building's ledge, and cocked its head, following the laugh's last seconds.

Moonlight glanced across its back, across its massive shoulders, down its craned, cabled neck, across its skull, striking a triangle at one pointed bat's ear.

It rose into space, its wings spread wide, then fell, its wings now a fluttering cape wrapped tight about the body of a man.

It fell past me, its shadow sliding across walls, growing to swallow whole buildings, lit by the clouds below.

The shadow faded into the clouds.

It was gone.

. . . the 80-page giant comic cost 25 cents, but I bought it anyway.

Frank Miller
Los Angeles 1988

FRANK MILLER

DC COMICS INC.

JENETTE KAHN
President and Publisher

DICK GIORDANO
V.P.–Executive Editor

DENNY O'NEIL
Editor–Original Series

RICHARD BRUNING
Editor–Collected Edition

TERRI CUNNINGHAM
Mgr.–Editorial Admin.

PAT BASTIENNE
Mgr.–Editorial Coord.

BOB ROZAKIS
Production Director

PAUL LEVITZ
Executive V.P.

JOE ORLANDO
V.P.–Creative Director

BRUCE BRISTOW
Marketing Director

MATT RAGONE
Circulation Director

PAT CALDON
Controller

Cover art: David Mazzucchelli
Cover design: Rian Hughes
Publication design: Janice Walker

BATMAN: YEAR ONE
ISBN 1 85286 077 4
Published by Titan Books Ltd.
58 St. Giles High St.
London WC2H 8LH

First Titan Edition: August 1988
10 9 8 7 6 5 4 3

He will become the
greatest crimefighter
the world has ever known...

It won't be easy.

CHAPTER ONE:
WHO I AM
HOW I COME TO BE

January 4

Gotham City.

Maybe it's all I deserve, now.

Maybe it's just my time in Hell.

Twelve hours. My stomach's been trying to eat itself for the last five.

Barbara's flying in. I don't care how much it costs.

Train's no way to come to Gotham...

...in an airplane, from above, all you'd see are the streets and buildings.

Fool you into thinking it's civilized.

...BEGINNING OUR FINAL DESCENT TO *GOTHAM CITY.* PLEASE RETURN SEATS AND TRAYS TO THEIR UPRIGHT POSITIONS...

From here, it's clean shafts of concrete and snowy rooftops. The work of men who died generations ago.

From here, it looks like an achievement.

I should have taken the train. I should be closer.

I should see the enemy.

By now Barbara's gotten her tests back. I only hate myself a little for hoping they came out negative.

This is no place to raise a family.

NICE *BOOK* FOR A SMALL *DONATION*--

NO, PLEASE--

GORDON!

LIEUTENANT JAMES *GORDON!*

NICE *BOOK*-- LOOK AT THE *PICTURES*-- GAA *

WALK, SKINHEAD.

NAME'S *FLASS,* LIEUTENANT. DETECTIVE *FLASS.* COMMISSIONER *LOEB* SENT ME TO MAKE SURE YOU DIDN'T MISS YOUR *APPOINTMENT* WITH HIM.

HOPE YOU DON'T MIND IF I CALL YOU *JIMMY.*

WELL, I --

NICE -- *koff* -- COLORS...

WELCOME TO *GOTHAM,* JIMMY. IT'S NOT AS BAD AS IT *LOOKS.* ESPECIALLY IF YOU'RE A *COP.*

COPS GOT IT *MADE* IN *GOTHAM.*

--WELCOME *HOME,* MR. WAYNE--

--HOW'S IT *FEEL* TO BE *BACK*--

--PRINCESS *CAROLINE*--

--ANY *PLANS,* MR. WAYNE--

--ANY TRUTH TO THE *RUMORS*--

THE TWENTY-FIVE-YEAR-OLD HEIR TO THE WAYNE MILLIONS DECLINED TO COMMENT ON RUMORS OF *ROMANCE* IN HIS LIFE...

...OR ON HIS *PLANS* ON HIS *RETURN* TO GOTHAM AFTER *TWELVE YEARS* ABROAD. WE'LL KEEP YOU *POSTED* ON GOTHAM'S *RICHEST*--AND BEST *LOOKING* -- NATIVE SON. TOM?

③

THANK YOU, JACKIE. FOLLOWING THE *DISAP-PEARANCE* OF A KEY *WITNESS,* ASSISTANT DISTRICT ATTORNEY *HARVEY DENT* HAS WITHDRAWN *CONSPIRACY* CHARGES AGAINST POLICE *COMMISSIONER LOEB...*

YOU KNOW WE'RE ALL *DELIGHTED* TO HAVE YOU ON THE *TEAM,* LIEUTENANT.

GILLIAN B. LOEB
COMMISSIONER OF POLICE

YOU'LL GET MY BEST WORK, SIR. I PROMISE.

AND WE ARE A *TEAM.* A *TEAM* NEEDS *TEAM SPIRIT,* DON'T YOU THINK?

YES IT DOES. AND YOUR *RECORD* SHOWS YOU'VE *GOT* WHAT IT *TAKES.*

I KNOW I'VE MADE MY *MISTAKES,* SIR. I'M *GRATEFUL* FOR THIS CHANCE TO *PROVE* MYSELF...

IF THERE'S ONE THING I CAN'T *STAND,* IT'S *SMOKING.*

WHAT *MISTAKES* HAVE *YOU* MADE, LIEUTENANT? YOU KEPT THE *MEDIA* AWAY FROM IT. THAT'S THE *BOTTOM LINE,* ISN'T IT?

YES IT IS.

I'D FEEL BETTER ABOUT TOUGH-ING OUT THE NICOTINE FIT...

...if I didn't have to smell those Eucalyptus Cough Drops of his...

I *SWEAR* YOU WON'T HAVE TO WORRY ABOUT MY *HONESTY,* COMMISSIONER.

LAST THING ON MY MIND. *LAST* THING.

ALFRED.

I TRUST YOU'VE BEEN *WELL,* MASTER BRUCE.

Wayne Manor.

Built as a fortress, generations past, to protect a fading line of royalty from an age of Equals.

Mother. Father. It's good to be back.

KNEW YOU'D LIKE THE COMMISSIONER, JIMMY.

AND HE'LL BE JUST AS GOOD TO *YOU* AS YOU ARE TO *HIM*, YOU CAN *COUNT* ON THAT...

I keep telling myself it's either this or pumping gas...

...then I tell myself I'm doing it for Barbara...

SCREEECHH

FLASS-- WHAT'S--

NOTHING I CAN'T HANDLE *SOLO*, JIMMY.

MOTHER KNOW YOU'RE HERE, STEVIE?

OH, *MAN*...

...NOT *DOING* ANYTH--

WHUKK

I keep talking to myself. This time I say you'd better know your facts before you bring another cop down.

Especially in public.

Flass has had Green Beret training. I can tell. And he knows how to use his size.

DEPT. OF SANITATI

I watch and I don't do a damn thing and I memorize every move.

For future reference.

⑤

WAS THAT *NECESSARY*?

HAD *THIS* LITTLE BEAUTY IN HIS *POCKET*.

IT'S A *COMB*, FLASS.

I'M ONLY *HUMAN*, JIMMY.

The tests.

I pray they're negative.

February 12

THE *BOYS*-- THEY'VE BEEN ASKING ME TO *TALK* TO YOU, JIMMY. THOUGHT MAYBE I COULD GET A *WORD* IN, KNOWING HOW *TIGHT* WE ARE.

THEY'RE *WORRIED* ABOUT YOU.

I'M *TOUCHED*, FLASS. BUT RIGHT NOW *I'M* WORRIED--ABOUT A *HOMICIDE*. TURN *LEFT*.

NEVER MAKE IT IN THIS BUSINESS IF YOU DON'T LEARN TO *RELAX*, JIMMY. I MEAN, WE'VE GOT OUR OWN WAY OF *DOING* THINGS, HERE IN GOTHAM.

I MEAN, YOU CAME DOWN PRETTY *HARD* ON MORGAN...

I MEAN, YOU WITH A *BABY* ON THE WAY...

CALL ME LIEUTENANT. MAKE YOUR NEXT *RIGHT*.

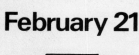

February 21

I'm not ready.

I have the means, the skill -- but not the method...

...no. That's not true. I have hundreds of methods.

But something's missing. Something isn't right.

I have to wait.

I have to wait.

February 26

...SO FATHER DONELLEY, HE SLIPS GORDON A *FIFTY* WITH THE *HANDSHAKE*...

GILLIAN B. L
COMMISSIONER OF POLICE

...AND *GORDON*, HE LOOKS AT IT LIKE HIS *HAND'S* GOT A *DISEASE.* THEN HE *THROWS* THE FIFTY IN THE PADRE'S *FACE.*

GIVES THE *SQUAD* A TWO-HOUR *LECTURE.* PUTS *SCHELL* ON *PROBATION.*

HE'S JUST NOT FIT-TING *IN*, GILL.

I HAD SUCH HOPES FOR THAT BOY...

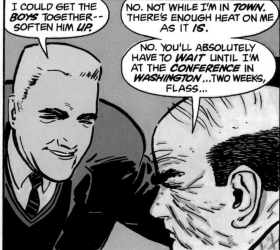

I COULD GET THE *BOYS* TOGETHER-- SOFTEN HIM *UP.*

NO. NOT WHILE I'M IN *TOWN.* THERE'S ENOUGH HEAT ON ME AS IT *IS.*

NO. YOU'LL ABSOLUTELY HAVE TO *WAIT* UNTIL I'M AT THE *CONFERENCE* IN *WASHINGTON* ...TWO WEEKS, FLASS...

March 11

The engine hums, gently, not quite convinced it should stop.

Everything is in place. The attendant was even obliging enough to ask me for my autograph. My alibi is set.

Bruce Wayne has been sighted at the same hotel as a visiting Hollywood sex queen. That should generate sufficient rumors--

--to account for my whereabouts for the next few hours.

This is a reconnaissance mission. Until I know more, I must avoid combat. Until I'm ready...

...my anonymity is an obvious priority. The murder of my parents is a matter of public record.

All it requires is a change in clothing and complexion--

--and a single, memorable, distracting detail.

Requested off this night shift four times now-- damn it, Barbara needs me at night these days, Barbara, and little James...

...so I hope it's a boy. So what.

Four times and no reply. I'm not making friends in the department--

GOING TO **WORK**, LIEUTENANT?

GOING TO BE **LATE**.

MAY HAVE TO SKIP THE WHOLE **NIGHT**.

It's a twenty block walk to the enemy camp.

It's been educational. I was sized up like a piece of meat by the leather boys in Robinson Park. I waded through pleas and half-hearted threats from junkies at the Finger Memorial. I stepped across a field of human rubble that lay sleeping in front of the overcrowded Sprang Mission.

Finally the worst of it.

The East End.

Hard to believe it's gotten worse.

CHEER YOU UP.

I DOUBT IT. HOW OLD ARE YOU?

YOUNG AS YOU WANT ME TO BE.

STUPID B-- THAS ALL WRONG, HOLLY. YOU DOIN' IT WRONG.

DID WHAT YOU SAID. JUST LIKE--

THAS RIGHT, HONEY. BUT YOU GOT TO PICK YOU TYPES. GOT TO KNOW WHICH ONES WANT WHAT YOU GOT.

THIS ONE'S NOT--

I HAVEN'T SAID, HAVE I?

THAT VICE I SMELL?

THAT CRAZY VET BIT-- THAS OLD, MAN.

I'M NOT THE POLICE. BELIEVE ME.

YOU STILL *HERE?* *TOLD* YOU TO *GO,* HOLLY.

HE HADN'T *SAID.*

WE TALK THIS OVER *LATER,* SWEET CHUNKS.

NO...

...I THINK YOU'RE *FINISHED* WITH HER.

I'm provoking him.

I really shouldn't.

MAN, YOU *PUSHIN.* YOU ON THE *EDGE.*

YOU LOOKIN' FOR A *NEW* SCAR. *THAS* RIGHT. JUS TELL ME *WHERE,* MAN...

OH. GEEZ... CAN'T BE *VICE.* WE'RE PAID *UP.* JUST SOME *IDIOT* OUT TO GET HIMSELF *KILLED.*

SELINA... DON'T STOP *NOW...*

SHUT UP, SKUNK.

YOU KNOW WHAT I HATE *MOST* ABOUT *MEN,* SKUNK?

PLEASE, SELINA... *TELL* ME... WHY YOU *HATE* US SO... OH, *PLEASE...*

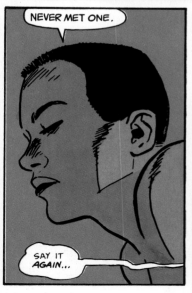

NEVER MET ONE.

SAY IT *AGAIN...*

His eyes keep flicking away from the girls to me. He turns away for a second --

-- a dead giveaway --

-- he's pretty fast --

--I won't say he has a chance--

--but he's fast.

This is getting a little too good to me-- better wrap it up--

XX ALL NIGHT TOPLESS

GIRLS GIRLS GIRLS !!!

Idiot--never should have done this--

--have to get out of here before I draw attention--

AAAA

COME ON YOU GUYS-- I GOT HIM--

Very good, Bruce.

You've really put the fear of God into them.

DAMN IT--

HEY--HE DIDN'T *MOVE*, MAN.

HE WAS *GOING* TO.

--hit an artery-- losing blood!--

--get up-- before they--

NEEDS A *DOCTOR*.

MAYBE AFTER HE'S *BOOKED*.

NNGG

--no-- can't let them--

can't

ANY *CASH*?

COUPLE BUCKS. NO I.D. ...

LOOK, MAN--

--HE'S *BLEEDING* ALL OVER THE *SEAT*. WE *GOT* TO TAKE HIM TO THE *HOSPITAL*.

YOU LOOK, BOY. I'VE RUN IN A *THOUSAND* LIKE HIM. *DRIFTERS*. WHO NEEDS THEM.

IF HE *DIES*, HE--

YOU TWO.

STOP THE CAR. GET OUT.

WHAT THE *HELL* ...

DON'T MIND *HIM*, BOY. PROBABLY *HOPPED UP* ON SOMETHING *FAST*, Y'KNOW?

I *WARNED* YOU.

OH MY *GOD*-- HE--

CHINKK

⑭

SMOKE FROM THE BLAZING *POLICE CRUISER* CAN BE SEEN FOR *BLOCKS*-- THE TWO *OFFICERS* WERE FOUND *UNCONSCIOUS*, THIRTY FEET AWAY...

HHNNGG

...made it...somehow... mustʼve made it here...to the car...

...hope I didnʼt...do anything stupid...getting here...

...done enough... wrong tonight...

...turn...the key, Bruce... isnʼt difficult...

...just a little... slippery...

They did just enough to keep me out of the hospital...

...canʼt let Barbara see me like this...

DETECTIVE *FLASS?* HEʼS *OFF DUTY*, LIEUTENANT. PROBABLY AT THE *POKER PARTY* OVER AT *CHUTEʼS.*

WITH THE *GUYS.*

The guys.

Maniac-- almost hit me--

--should arrest the clown--no way to treat a Porsche--

...God... fear of God...

THAT'S BRUCE WAYNE'S CAR. WHAT'S HE ON?

COCAINE. RICH PEOPLE TAKE COCAINE.

SAW A SPECIAL ON IT.

...fear...

...I have to make them afraid...

Dodging the Porsche gives me enough adrenalin to make the drive to Bay Ridge.

The bruises are starting to form and my spine feels fused when Wilson says good-bye to the guys.

Of course Wilson's the first to leave. Doesn't want to make his wife stay up too late waiting for him.

And he still has his girlfriend to see tonight.

Twenty minutes later Stannsen stumbles out, hunched over like he's lost his life savings.

Then Renny.

I let them both go home.

I don't crack his skull.

I don't crush his larynx.

I don't break his ribs or punch my hand through his chest.

I do just enough--

--to keep him out of the hospital.

I toss his gun into the woods. It should be rusty by morning.

I take his clothes off and leave him in his own cuffs by the side of the road.

He'll never report it. Not Flass. He'll make up some story that involves at least ten attackers and never admit I did it.

But he'll know. And he'll stay away from Barbara.

Thanks, Flass.

You've shown me what it takes to be a cop in Gotham City.

He has trained and
planned and waited
eighteen years.

He thinks he's ready...

CHAPTER TWO:
WAR IS
DECLARED

April 4

The day starts early with a call from Merkel about a hostage situation in Brigham Circle.

Barbara wakes up with me -- she always does, no matter how quiet I try to be -- and somehow has my coffee ready by the time I pull on my pants.

COME *IN*, MERKEL...

The rain has worked its magic on the wiring of my heap. Between Rice Krispy sounds I get every fourth word.

I'm two blocks from the action, my stomach lurching with the engine through backed-up traffic.

Damn rubberneckers...

NO CAN'T DON'T *WANT* ISN'T *BLANK*

Best I can tell, nobody's sure what the kidnapper wants. He isn't making much sense.

He's holding three children at gunpoint. Sounds like Merkel's got some background on him...

...I SAID *NO*, SIR. HE HASN'T FIRED A *SHOT*...

...*NO*, SIR, NOT A *CRIMINAL* RECORD. GOT THE WORD FROM *ARKHAM ASYLUM* ...YES, SIR. *ARKHAM*...

...NAME'S *ALBERT BLUME*. DIAGNOSED *PARANOID SCHIZOPHRENIC*, RELEASED *TWO WEEKS* AGO...

=SKRKK= NO, SIR -- NO =SKRKK= OF VIOLENT =SKRKK=

SIR -- TROUBLE -- IT'S =SKRKK=

=SKRKK= BRANDEN =SKRKK=

WORLD'S GREATEST DAD

Branden.

JESUS, YOU --

Coffee splashes in my lap, taking the last of the cotton from my mind.

Branden. Him and his lunatic gestapo.

It'll be a massacre.

WE'RE NOT HERE TO *ARGUE*, MERKEL. WE'RE HERE TO *CLEAN THINGS UP*.

AND I DON'T SEE A *SIGN* OF YOUR SOFT-HEARTED *LIEUTENANT GORDON*--

OH, NO...

Last month Branden and his swat team calmed down a riot in Robinson Park.

Didn't even leave the statues standing.

POLIC

ALMOST *HIT ME*--

WHAT THE--

-- CAN'T *SEE* WHAT'S--

DEFRIBBILATE.

DOESN'T *SMELL* OFTEN. TOO MANY *GUNS*.

Those kids don't have a chance--he'll push that poor bastard over the edge--

GORDON...

GO FIND YOUR *OWN* WAR, BRANDEN. OR I'LL HAVE YOU UP ON *CHARGES*.

WHFF

OH *MAN* IT'S GORDON--

WHERE'D HE--

I take the ugly weight off my hip...

...I hold it up like a dead rat and pray that the man understands...

Behind me Branden curses.

I head for the front door.

I'm sure nobody can see my knees wobble.

I hope Barbara isn't watching.

I know she is.

LIEUTENANT GORDON HAS *ENTERED* THE BUILDING--NO *SHOTS* YET...

The stairs creak, too loudly. A sneeze that's been building for twenty minutes just keeps threatening.

My nose drips. I don't have the nerve to wipe it.

The little girl is crying.

SPIDER NASTY DON'T *NOISE* IT--

--NO *LUNCH*. NO *LUNCH*.

I'LL ORDER OUT.

My shoes are full of icy rain. My feet are warm, compared to my stomach.

SAID *NO LUNCH* NO GANGRENE *LUNCH*.

I KNOW, I KNOW...

NO GANGR--

Poor kids must've been scared out of their wits.

Right. Like I wasn't.

April 5

HUMILIATED ME. IN FRONT OF MY *MEN*. *HUMILIATED* ME.

NOTHING BUT *TROUBLE*, THAT ONE.

YOU DO KNOW I *SYMPATHIZE*, DON'T YOU, BRANDEN?

GILLIAN B. L
COMMISSIONER
OF POLICE

YES YOU DO. AND YOU KNOW I'D LIKE *NOTHING* BETTER THAN TO *REMOVE* HIM FROM SERVICE. MY GOOD FRIEND DETECTIVE FLASS HAS MADE *SEVERAL* SUGGESTIONS ALONG THESE LINES.

BUT WE MUST BE *PATIENT*. GORDON HAS THE *PRESS* ON HIS SIDE...

HERO COP

STOP

It kicks.

Gunpowder burns my eyes and fills my nostrils.

A wad of lead flies...

If that were a man--

--the wad would shatter his spine and he'd feel his legs go dead even as his heart explodes...

Another kick.

The wad would leave a neat, round hole and I'd see the horror in his eyes as it pushed half his brain through the back of his skull.

I hate the gun.

I hate my job.

I keep practicing.

April 6

Another kick.

Strong boy, little James...

...I pray he's very strong. And smart enough to stay alive.

How did I let this happen?

How did I screw up so badly...to bring an innocent child to life...

...in a city without hope...

April 9

They call it my night off.

It starts out well enough, with the smell of Barbara's lemon chicken--

--and her fingers, kneading baby oil into my shoulders...

...Rachmaninoff, played soft...her idea...corny, but it works...

DON'T HAVE TO GO TO METROPOLIS...

...FOR A MAN OF STEEL...

...COULD USE A JACKHAMMER ON YOUR BACK...

FEELS GREAT, HONEY...

RINGG

...SAID YOU'D UNPLUG IT, JIM...

HONEY, I FORGOT... I'M SORRY...

YES, SERGEANT.

MAYBE YOU SHOULD CALL THE ZOO.

ALL RIGHT, ALL RIGHT, I'LL GET HIM.

IT'S MERKEL.

SOMETHING ABOUT A GIANT BAT.

CHICKEN WILL KEEP.

--twist it--

--make it count--

--I pull a limp body up...

--the television hits--

...good thing he blacked out... if he'd kept thrashing...

...my shoulder... and teeth... are still where they belong...

...lucky.

Lucky amateur.

May 15

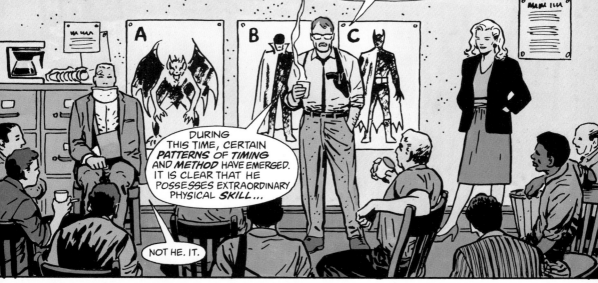

IF WE CAN STOP BEING *HYSTERICAL* FOR A MOMENT, GENTLEMEN.

OUR *VIGILANTE* --OR *BATMAN*, AS HE'S CALLED-- HAS APPARENTLY COMMITTED SEVENTY-EIGHT ACTS OF *ASSAULT* IN THE PAST FIVE WEEKS.

DURING THIS TIME, CERTAIN *PATTERNS* OF *TIMING* AND *METHOD* HAVE EMERGED. IT IS CLEAR THAT HE POSSESSES EXTRAORDINARY PHYSICAL *SKILL*...

NOT HE. IT.

YOU'VE GOT SOMETHING TO *CONTRIBUTE*, DETECTIVE FLASS?

HE'S NOT HUMAN. I'M JUST TELLING YOU HE'S NOT HUMAN.

THANK YOU, DETECTIVE FLASS.

WHILE THE VIGILANTE HAS BEEN CAREFUL TO REMAIN UNPREDICTABLE, CHOOSING THE NEIGHBORHOODS FOR HIS ASSAULTS AT RANDOM--

--HE CONSISTENTLY OPERATES BETWEEN THE HOURS OF MIDNIGHT AND FOUR A.M....

...ANYBODY GOT A MATCH?

THANK YOU, DETECTIVE ESSEN.

HE'S WORKING HIS WAY FROM STREET LEVEL CRIME TO ITS UPPER ECHELONS, FROM JUNKIE MUGGER TO PUSHER TO SUPPLIER--

--AND, ALONG THE WAY, TO ANY COPS THAT MIGHT BE HELPING THE WHOLE PROCESS ALONG...

...NOW, FLASS. TELL US WHAT YOU KNOW ABOUT BATMAN.

TRY NOT TO EXAGGERATE.

IT'S LIKE MY REPORT, LIEUTENANT. I RECEIVED AN ANONYMOUS TIP LEADING ME TO AN EAST END COCAINE DELIVERY...

"...I was in the process of single-handedly apprehending the felons," says Flass, and coughs.

He looks around the room to see if anybody's going to challenge him, and goes on...

..."then I heard giant wings flap. It flew down from the sky--"

Somebody chuckles. Flass turns another shade redder.

"--its wings were about thirty feet across. It bellowed like...well, I've never heard anything like it..."

"...one of the felons I had not yet disarmed produced a 357 magnum--"

"--he fired--point blank range, at the creature--"

"--and the bullet passed straight through the creature like it wasn't there--"

The snorts and giggles stop Flass cold for a second. He shoots me a look I'd like to frame and put on my wall.

"--and it started laughing..."

"...Other members of the gang drew forth their guns--something flew from the creature's hand."

"I remember noticing it had claws..."

CLAWS. RIGHT.

...IT WAS LITTLE DART THINGS...THEY PARALYZED THE FELONS...

...LITTLE DART THINGS...

...BUT ME HE SINGLED OUT...

GENTLEMEN, GENTLEMEN...

GO ON, FLASS. PLEASE.

May 19

The costume--and the weapons--have been tested. It's time to get serious.

Chauffeur by chauffeur, I make my way toward the Mayor's mansion...

Only three of them are awake.

Only half of them are armed.

PFFT

There's a guard with a machine pistol in the yard...

LIEUTENANT GORDON. WHAT A PLEASANT SURPRISE.

BATMAN? I AM EATING, LIEUTENANT.

...NO, I HAVE NOT FILLED YOUR REQUESTS FOR PERSONNEL. I FIND THEM EXCESSIVE.

...YES, LIEUTENANT, I AM WELL AWARE OF HOW MANY LAWS THE VIGILANTE IS BREAKING. BUT THERE ARE TWO SIDES TO EVERYTHING, AREN'T THERE?

Lieutenant Gordon. I've been hearing his name often.

All the right people seem to hate him.

Flood's all set...

YES THERE ARE. AND THE BATMAN IS HAVING A POSITIVE EFFECT ON PUBLIC SPIRIT. OR HAVE YOU NOTICED THE DROP IN STREET CRIME THESE PAST WEEKS?...

...FURTHER, I AM NOT IN THE HABIT OF EXPLAINING MYSELF TO MY LIEUTENANTS.

I HOPE WE UNDERSTAND EACH OTHER, GORDON.

HAVE YOU SEEN BATMAN, COMMISSIONER? THEY SAY HE'S HUGE...

YOU SHOULDN'T PRY, MARIAN. GILL HAS HIS HANDS FULL, THESE DAYS.

WE'RE TRUSTING HIM TO COPE WITH BATMAN-- AND WITH GORDON.

AND I APPRECIATE YOUR TRUST, BOYS. YES I DO.

GOOD TO SEE YOU ALL. IT'S BEEN A WHILE...

Not yet...

HELL, GILL. NOBODY WAS ABOUT TO COME NEAR *YOU* UNTIL THE *POLLS* WERE IN ON THE *BATMAN* THING.

DON'T GO CHEAP ON THE *WINE*, MARIAN.

CHARLIE. THE THINGS YOU SAY.

THE *COUNCILMAN* IS *BLUNT* ABOUT HIS *CONCERNS*. THIS *IS* AN *ELECTION* YEAR.

MY ORGANIZATION IS *LIKEWISE* CONCERNED, COMMISSIONER. BATMAN IS COSTING US *MONEY*.

TWO *SIDES* TO *EVERYTHING*, FRIENDS. LOOK AT THE *LONG TERM*. A FEW *STREET* OPERATORS ARE PUT OUT OF ACTION, YES--

--BUT THE *PEOPLE* OF *GOTHAM CITY* HAVE A *HERO*. MAKES THEM FEEL *SAFE*. AND THE *SAFER* THEY FEEL, THE FEWER *QUESTIONS* THEY ASK.

I DON'T LIKE IT. IT'S STIRRING THINGS *UP*.

THAT KID *DENT* IS PUSHING *INTERNAL AFFAIRS* TO GO AFTER DETECTIVE *FLASS*.

FLASS WOULD BE *DIFFICULT* TO *REPLACE*. AND, SHOULD HE *TALK*...

DENT IS *YOUR* PROBLEM, FALCONE. YES HE IS.

...*now*.

WHAT THE HELL--

WHO THE--

GOD WE'LL ALL *DIE*--

THE *LIGHTS* WHAT HAPPENED TO THE *LIGHTS*--

Now--take out the wall--

--hit the flood--

--it's showtime--

SETTLE *DOWN* DAMN IT IT'S JUST *SMOKE*--

SOME STUPID *PRANK*--

POISON IT'S--

SHUT UP--

POOMM

May 20

-- NO *EXCUSES*, GORDON. THAT *VIGILANTE* GOES *UNDER* -- *INSTANTLY* -- OR IT'S YOUR *JOB!*

GILLIAN B

COMMIS

...YES, SIR...

June 2

She knows how to walk in *heels.*

So few women do, these days. It's practically a lost art.

And she knows how to scream. You could hear it from the rooftops.

Normally, screaming wouldn't help. Not in this neighborhood.

Here on the East End, a midnight walk constitutes attempted suicide.

Lucky for her that there are so many cops around.

There's Sergeant Feck, playing *who...*

And hunched in that sedan-- Detectives Shelly and Lerner.

There are six more officers waiting, crouched in stoops and garbage dumpers, down the block.

COFFEE

Gordon's wasting a lot of manpower on these traps.

(39)

June 5

SIR-- YOUR *ROLLS* -- IT'S *GONE*--

SIR--

IT WAS *HIM*. SAID THE *ROLLS* IS IN THE *RIVER*. EVEN TOLD ME WHICH *PIER*.

THINKS HE'S A DAMNED *ROBIN HOOD*.

HE *DIES*.

June 6

HE KNOWS *WHEN* AND *WHERE* WE SET OUR *TRAPS* FOR HIM--

--AND NIGHT BY *NIGHT*, HE *TERRORIZES* THE MOST *POWERFUL* MEN IN *GOTHAM*. YOU HEARD WHAT HE DID TO THE *ROMAN'S* CAR?

LAUGHED MYSELF *SILLY*, LIEUTENANT. A *ROLLS ROYCE*...

YES --YOU'VE BEEN AFTER THE *ROMAN* FOR *YEARS*, FROM WHAT I HEAR. ACTUALLY CAME CLOSE TO *INDICTING* HIM, ONCE OR TWICE.

SOME OF YOUR WITNESSES CHANGE THEIR *TESTIMONY*. THE REST *VANISH*. IT MUST BE *FRUSTRATING*.

OH, YES.

I UNDERSTAND HE'S USED HIS *MUSCLE* TO KEEP YOU AN *ASSISTANT* DISTRICT ATTORNEY...

≈WHFF≈ YOU KEEP IN *SHAPE*, DON'T YOU, MR. DENT?

WHAT ARE YOU *DRIVING* AT, LIEUTENANT?

I NEED TO KNOW WHERE YOU WERE ON THE FOLLOWING DATES ...

...THOUGHT HE'D NEVER LEAVE.

YOU CAN COME OUT NOW.

ALIBIS? DENT HAD ONE ALIBI, ESSEN. FOR EVERY DATE.

SAYS HE WAS HOME BETWEEN MIDNIGHT AND FOUR. WITH HIS WIFE. NO POINT IN QUESTIONING HER.

YOU REALLY THINK HE'S BATMAN, LIEUTENANT?

IT'S POSSIBLE. DENT CERTAINLY IS PASSIONATE ENOUGH.

BUT IT'D TAKE MORE THAN MUSCLES TO FIGHT THE WAY BATMAN DOES--OR TO GET AROUND THE WAY HE DOES. AND THOSE WEAPONS...

...I MEAN, HE'S GOT AN ARSENAL. HARD TO AFFORD ON DENT'S SALARY.

MONEY-- LIEUTENANT... BRUCE WAYNE IS THE RICHEST MAN IN GOTHAM--AND--

--BEING FROM OUT OF TOWN, YOU MIGHT NOT KNOW THIS, BUT HIS PARENTS WERE MURDERED. BY A MUGGER, I THINK.

HE WAS JUST A LITTLE BOY AT THE TIME ...

I COULD KISS YOU, ESSEN.

I'm already tasting her lipstick on the cigarette...

...her fingernails bite into my knee--

--that truck-- what the hell--

SKREEEEEE

Maybe it's pills--

--maybe it's a heart attack--

--maybe it's both, but that doesn't matter--

--he's out of control-- his foot must be pressed to the accelerator--

--oh, no-- that old woman--

--can't let this happen--

SKREEEEEEE

--come on you heap move--

LIEUTENANT--

TAKE THE WHEEL.

K BLAMM
KBLAMM

--SAVED THAT OLD **WOMAN**... HE...

They think--I attacked those cops--opening up--

--catch a bullet in my leg--

--ignore it--

Blind alley-- no way out--

--except that window--

--only chance--

--buy me a moment--

NO ONE **FIRES** WITHOUT MY **ORDER**--

--GET THE **FRONT** OF THAT PLACE COVERED--

--MERKEL-- TAKE A SQUAD TO THE **ROOF**--

LIEUTENANT--IT'S THE **COMMISSIONER**--

--the roof--if I can reach it before they do--

--before they get air support--

--COMMISSIONER, THERE'S NO **NEED** FOR--

--**BATMAN** HASN'T ATTACKED **ANYBODY**--

--COMMISSIONER-- YOU CAN'T LET **BRANDEN**--

They've got him CORNERED.
They've got him OUTNUMBERED.
They've got him TRAPPED.

They're in TROUBLE...

CHAPTER THREE:
BLACK DAWN

June 7

nffmgmm

GO WAY, OTTO. YOU DON' EAT FR 'N' HOUR.

MROWW

mmfgg

SIAMESE. TOO NOISY. SHOULD'VE LEFT YOU AT THE MARKET.

WHOLE CREW NOW. GANGING UP. IT'S MUTINY.

HOLLY. WHAT THE HELL TIME IS IT?

SELINA-- OUTSIDE--

RROWNRRRWREOWW RROWW

VOGUE

--EXPLOSIONS--

ggnf

CHRIST. NOT EVEN LIGHT OUT.

CHRIST. FIVE IN THE MORNING.

MMREEEOWW

MRROWWWRRR

I'M BEING SERIOUS, SELINA. THINGS ARE BLOWING UP OVER BY ROBINSON PARK.

MAYBE BRANDEN'S CORNERED A JAYWALKER.

TURN THE TV ON, HOLLY. GOT TO HAVE SOMETHING ON THIS...

The fifth load goes up. I pray it'll be the last.

He will be soon, anyway. Branden and the collection of sociopaths he calls a swat team will see to that.

Commissioner's orders. That's what Branden told me.

The Police Commissioner of Gotham City wants a corpse.

THIS IS UNIT *THREE*-- WE ARE APPROACHING *TARGET* AREA--

WATCH WHERE YOU'RE *GOING*, YOU--

NO *PRISONERS*, MEN.

LIEUTENANT *GORDON*-- YOU SHOULDN'T BE *STANDING* JUST YET.

I'M ALL RIGHT...

Batman. He's made enemies of every criminal in Gotham--and nearly every elected official.

They've only got him cornered because he got hurt saving an old woman's life. They--

--I mean *we*, of course...

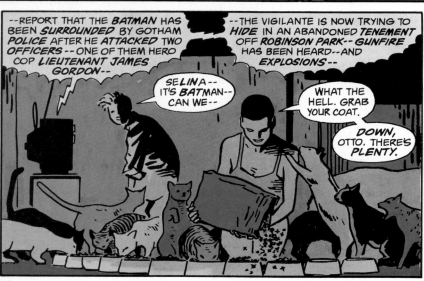

--REPORT THAT THE *BATMAN* HAS BEEN *SURROUNDED* BY GOTHAM POLICE AFTER HE *ATTACKED* TWO OFFICERS -- ONE OF THEM HERO COP *LIEUTENANT JAMES GORDON*--

--THE VIGILANTE IS NOW TRYING TO *HIDE* IN AN ABANDONED *TENEMENT* OFF *ROBINSON PARK*-- GUNFIRE HAS BEEN HEARD--AND EXPLOSIONS--

SELINA-- IT'S *BATMAN*-- CAN WE--

WHAT THE HELL. GRAB YOUR COAT.

DOWN, OTTO. THERE'S *PLENTY*.

--NOW THERE IS TENSE *SILENCE*--EYEWITNESSES SAY A HEAVILY ARMED *SWAT TEAM* OF EIGHTEEN MEN HAS ENTERED THE BUILDING--

BRAKABRAKABRA

SIR--HE'S TAKEN OUT UNIT *THREE*...THE WHOLE UNIT, COMMISSIONER...

THIS WILL NOT DO. THIS WILL NOT DO AT ALL.

WHAT'S WRONG WITH OUR *MARKSMAN*? I TRUST YOU DIDN'T GET ME A BLIND *MARKSMAN*, DID YOU?

NO, SIR. HE'S OUR BEST MAN. BUT THERE ARE A HUNDRED PLACES TO *HIDE* IN THERE--

--UNTIL THE *SUN* IS HIGHER IN THE *SKY*. IT WON'T BE LONG, SIR...

The only other survivor of the attack shares a shrinking shadow with me.

I owe him an apology.

I've made a mess of things. Let it all get out of hand.

The enemy is closing in, relentless, unstoppable...

...through a crack in the wall I look at him.

With my belt, I lost my rope, my thermite, my tear gas -- even my batarangs.

I'm down to the blowgun in my boot--

KREEE

STEP IT UP--

CAREFUL-- STAIRS ARE GIVING--

RREEOOWWWW

WHAT THE HELL--

JUST A CAT, MAN--

IT'S A BAT WE'RE AFTER--

KEEP AN EYE OUT--

Knew he wouldn't stay quiet.

Siamese.

Down to the blowgun and its three darts--

--and an unofficial invention of Wayne Electronics.

Haven't tested it for this great a distance. Or for use in daylight.

Too bad I can't afford to patent it. I'd make a fortune.

But then, I already have a fortune...

...if I didn't, I couldn't have built the device.

If my family manor weren't placed over a huge cave...

...the Batcave, I call it.

It's full of bats.

Extraordinary creatures, bats. Nearly blind--

--they are sensitive to a range of sound far beyond our hearing.

Took me weeks to find an ultrasonic tone that attracts them.

All of them.

SKEE SKEE SKEE

Wayne Manor is miles from Gotham. They'll take a few minutes to get here--

--should things go well.

Wait... wait...

...let them waste all the time they want...

KEEEOOOWWRRR

STEADY, MAN--JUST THAT CAT AGAIN--

--GETTING ON MY NERVES--

WHFF WHOEVER BATMAN IS -- HE'S STRONGER THAN A...

QUIET -- HE COULD BE NFFGNN ANYWHERE...

SAID HE WAS IN THE CHIMNEY -- THERE --

HOLD IT, YOU IDIOT --

DROP THAT BEAM -- THEY WEREN'T QUICK ENOUGH -- THEY'RE USELESS --

-- WE'RE LUCKY HE DIDN'T KILL THEM --

-- NOW FAN OUT -- YOU'RE LEAVING YOURSELVES WIDE OP

HHKKK

The slightest dose of Anaconda on the darts -- enough to put a man to sleep --

BRAKA BRAKA BRAKA BRAKA

-- for a day or so --

-- twelve men left -- two darts --

-- no good --

-- one bullet -- will make all the difference --

-- they've got thousands --

SPAKK

GOT HIM--

--GET IN *CLOSE*-- CUT THAT BASTARD IN *HALF*--

--*GOT* HIM, MAN, WE'VE *GOT* HIM--

Groggy-- losing-- too much blood--

--had to-- put a bullet-- in my good leg-- didn't they--

KKRAAAKKK

--forget it-- ignore it--

--put what's left into it--

YOU'RE THE ONE--

61

—WHO TRIED TO SHOOT THE *CAT*—

≤KOFF≥ CAN'T *SEE*—

HH*WHFFF*

BRAKK

CAN'T *MOVE*—GET ME *OUT*—

The crowd is all screams and angry shouts. Then, I hear a wrecking ball take out the wall—

—and a hardware store clatter across the street.

A cheer goes up. They've made a hero out of him.

Then the cheering disintegrates...

...and the screaming starts again...

THWOKK

—ART— GET OUT OF THE *WAY*—

—LOOK—

WHAT THE *HELL*—

—UP THERE—

—MY *GOD*—

—MY *GOD*—

MY LORD, WHAT'S--

THERE-- DOWN THERE-- HE'S GOT A MOTORCYCLE-- GET AFTER HIM OR I'LL HAVE YOU SHOT--

--GET AFTER HIM--

Commissioner Loeb chased a cloud of bats for twelve blocks. When the cloud broke up, he found out that was all he was chasing.

Somewhere along the way the Batman must've taken a turn--and told his pets to keep going.

Always eager to please the Commissioner, Detective Swanson pursued the bats to the bitter end...

...and, speaking of bitter ends...

...every member of Branden's team, every cop, and everybody in the crowd were vaccinated for their bat bites.

Never have so many had so much trouble sitting down.

The owner of a nearby men's store opened up his shop, four hours later, to find a three-piece suit missing--

--and payment for it sitting on his cash register.

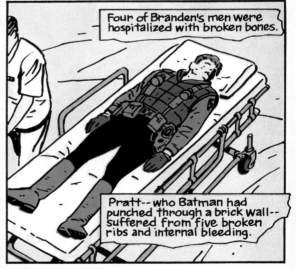

Four of Branden's men were hospitalized with broken bones.

Pratt--who Batman had punched through a brick wall-- suffered from five broken ribs and internal bleeding.

The dead winos had no relatives to complain about their firebombing.

Everyone who would've ordered Branden or Loeb up on charges remains unavailable to me by appointment or phone...

June 9

...as has my prime suspect in this case-- Bruce Wayne, the richest man in Gotham City.

Sgt. Essen informed me that Wayne's parents were murdered by a mugger when he was six years old. That's enough motive, I suppose, to make a man dress like Dracula and assault criminals...

...and save cats...

...Wayne's butler informed me that his boss has been skiing in Switzerland for six weeks.

I squeezed permission for an international call from Captain Pierce...

...I've had easier root canals-- you'd think Pierce was paying for the call out of his own pocket...

...and I spoke to somebody in Switzerland who said he was Bruce Wayne--

--then told me he'd taken a nasty spill on the slopes--broken both legs and one arm--

--but assured me he'd be back in the country in a month. Said he'd be happy to talk with me. Laughed when I mentioned Batman.

Asked me for his autograph.

WAYNE COULD AFFORD AN *IMPERSONATOR*-- AND *CASTS* ON HIS *ARM* AND *LEGS* WOULD COVER *BULLET WOUNDS*--EXACTLY WHERE *BATMAN* RECEIVED THEM...

...I'M SORRY, ESSEN. DID YOU SAY SOMETHING?

WORLD'S GREATEST DAD

June 17

SELINA-- YOU PUNCHED STAAN--

WE'RE CHANGING OUR LINE OF *WORK*, HOLLY.

I GOT AN *IDEA*.

It's getting to be a habit for Essen and I to have a cup of coffee at the local diner before calling it a night.

Actually, I'm the only one who has coffee--she goes for herb tea--she'd qualify as a health nut if she didn't smoke...

...we stay longer tonight, hoping to wait out the rain. We run out of shop talk, but keep going...

...turns out her first name is Sarah and her family is from Germany, a generation back. She's got a thing about the bad rap that Germans generally get.

She got into law enforcement after being told she was too masculine for about six other careers.

Whoever told her she was masculine must've been blind, deaf, and dead.

The rain's eased up and I'm an hour late and feeling terrible about having forgotten to call Barbara when we decide to risk it and look for a cab.

A group of bikers notice Essen's legs and make the usual remarks.

We ignore them and keep walking.

Turns out she's from Chicago, some years back. Small world.

Even went to the same place for ribs. I'm sure I would've noticed her...

...though, come to think of it, she was probably in high school then...

...Gotham weather. Just when the rain seems to be clearing up, lightning flashes--

--and we learn how Noah felt. Not having an ark, we settle for a doorway.

A cab comes. She takes it. We don't say good night.

August 7

I DON'T KNOW, SELINA-- I MEAN, YOU SPENT ALL OUR MONEY ON THAT COSTUME--

I MEAN, IT'S PRETTY QUEER--

I MEAN--

IT'S MONEY, HOLLY. BE A KICK. JUST WATCH.

SELINA--

I hate this city.

I hate myself and the night and everything it brings.

Mostly, I hate it when she cries...

...another fight. We fight so much, Barbara and I. She tells me I'm away too much and just when I should apologize, I snap at her... I freeze up inside...

...tonight, she called the office and I wasn't there-- I was out having coffee with Sarah--

--Sarah--my God, I'm calling her Sarah now... it's all wrong...

...and Barbara's right, as always...

He's out to clean
up a city that
likes being dirty.

He can't do it alone.

CHAPTER FOUR:
FRIEND IN NEED

September 2

It's the right thing to do.

It's the only thing to do.

YOU SHOULD TAKE THE BRACELET. I'M SURE YOUR WIFE WOULD LIKE IT.

NO. PLEASE, SARAH. KEEP IT.

DAMN IT, JIM. YOU'RE RIGHT, OF COURSE.

I JUST WANT TO *KNOW*-- IF YOUR WIFE WEREN'T *PREGNANT,* WOULD YOU--

--I'M SORRY. WASN'T FAIR.

DAMN IT, JIM.

HERO COP LIEUTENANT *JAMES GORDON* TODAY APPREHENDED NOTORIOUS NARCOTICS DEALER *JEFFERSON SKEEVERS.* IT LOOKS LIKE *GORDON'S* OUT TO SET A *RECORD.* RIGHT, TOM?

IT SURE DOES, TRISH. HE'S CAUGHT A *BIG* FISH THIS TIME. IF SKEEVERS IS *CONVICTED,* THIS'LL BE THE *FOURTH* TIME HE GOES TO PRISON. BET THEY THROW AWAY THE *KEY.*

September 7

Her arms are strong. Her whole body's strong.

It's late. We've both worked late again.

I never get tired around her.

She's requested a transfer. She's leaving Gotham City.

I'm in love with her.

It's the only thing to do.

JUDGE RAFFERTY SET *BAIL* FOR *JEFFERSON SKEEVERS.* SURPRISINGLY, ASSISTANT DISTRICT ATTORNEY *HARVEY DENT* DID NOT *ARGUE* WITH THIS DECISION...

September 10

I *KNOW* YOU AREN'T ON THE *TAKE*-- AND I DON'T *THINK* YOU'RE *CRAZY*--

--SO TELL ME *WHY* YOU LET THEM LET *SKEEVERS* OUT ON THE *STREET,* DENT--

I UNDERSTAND HOW YOU *FEEL,* LIEUTENANT.

WOULD YOU LIKE TO BORROW MY *UMBRELLA?*

September 11

NO. NO. NONE OF THAT. YOU STAY *CLEAN* UNTIL WE'VE GOTTEN YOU *OFF.*

DON'T SWEAT IT, BABE. JUST A COUPLE OF *LINES.*

DENT AND *GORDON* ARE *HOT* FOR YOU, SKEEVERS. THEY'D *LOVE* TO CATCH YOU WITH YOUR PANTS DOWN.

CATCH ME? THEY *CAUGHT* ME, BABE-- AND THEY LET ME *GO.* AND *YOU* GOT ME A *COURT ORDER* TYING *GORDON'S* HANDS...

NNFF

September 12

September 13

DETECTIVE *FLASS* IS A *FRIEND* OF MINE, GORDON. YOU MIGHT HAVE AT LEAST *INFORMED* ME OF YOUR PLANS BEFORE HANDING HIS HEAD TO *INTERNAL AFFAIRS.*

IT WAS A *SLIP,* SIR. EVERYBODY'S WORKING SUCH LONG HOURS.

GILLIAN B. L
COMMISSIONER
OF POLICE

FRIENDSHIP, GORDON. *LOYALTY.* THESE WORDS STILL *COUNT* FOR SOMETHING IN *GOTHAM CITY.*

WE TOOK *YOU* IN. YES WE DID. BLEMISHES AND ALL. AND YOU *DO* HAVE YOUR *BLEMISHES.* AND YOU GO AND --

I'VE DONE EXACTLY WHAT I PROMISED, COMMIS-SIONER. YOU GET MY BEST WORK.

STOP

YOU GET GOOD *PRESS,* I'LL GIVE YOU THAT.

THEY *LIKE* YOU, DON'T THEY, *AGEE* AND HIS PACK AT THE *GAZETTE.*

BUT THEY DON'T *KNOW* YOU. NO THEY DON'T.

NOT THE WAY *WE* KNOW YOU.

TERRIBLE IF THEY-- OR YOUR *WIFE*-- LEARNED OF THE *SPECIAL NATURE* OF YOUR *RELATIONSHIP*--

-- WITH SERGEANT *ESSEN.*

WALLS HAVE *EARS,* JIMMY.

September 25

COMMISSIONER LOEB ASSURES GOTHAM THAT THE MANHUNT FOR THE *BATMAN* CONTINUES, WITH HERO COP *JAMES GORDON* ON THE CASE...

The butler makes us feel as welcome as a virus. He leads us through a few dozen rooms the size of small states to Wayne's study.

Wayne's been out of the country. Wayne's had the flu. This morning I was told he had a hangover, but he'd see me.

Better than having Barbara stay at home and worry about being so overdue...

POLICE LIEUTENANT AND MRS. *GORDON*, SIR.

MRS. GORDON. I'M CHARMED.

ALFRED--BE A JOY AND GET SOME *GLASSES* FOR OUR *GUESTS*.

AND ANOTHER *BOTTLE*. THIS ONE'S *EVAPORATED*.

LITTLE *EARLY* IN THE DAY FOR US, THANKS.

MR. WAYNE--I DON'T WANT TO WASTE YOUR *TIME*...

MY TIME IS *WORTHLESS*, LIEUTENANT. JUST ASK *ALFRED*.

HMF.

I'VE BEEN FOLLOWING YOUR *EXPLOITS*, LIEUTENANT, AND I MUST SAY THAT I'M *IMPRESSED*. YOU'RE GETTING AS MUCH PRESS AS *BATMAN*.

IT IS *BATMAN* YOU WANT TO TALK ABOUT, ISN'T IT? SOMETHING ABOUT MY *BEING* HIM?

EXCUSE ME. IT MUST BE THE *CHAMPAGNE*. I NEGLECTED TO INTRODUCE MY *FRIEND* -- YOU SEE, I'M NOT SURE OF HER *NAME*, AND SHE DOESN'T SPEAK ANY LANGUAGE *I* KNOW...

THAT MUST BE CONVENIENT.

BARBARA.

MR. WAYNE, I NEED TO KNOW WHERE YOU WERE ON THE FOLLOWING DATES...

He laughs and rings for his butler. His butler brings his datebook.

I could auction off the phone numbers in his datebook for a fortune.

They're all women. They're all famous. They're all beautiful.

HE'S A *PIG*, JIM.

HE'S *ACTING* LIKE ONE, THAT'S FOR SURE ... BUT...

...BUT ANY MAN WHO'D WEAR A *CAPE*-- AND IT'S A *CAPE*, NOT WINGS, I'VE SEEN IT--

--ANYBODY WHO'D WEAR A *CAPE* AND HUNT *CRIMINALS* MIGHT GO PRETTY *FAR* TO KEEP HIS *SECRETS*...

... SECRETS. DAMN IT ALL...

JIM -- WHY ARE YOU *STOPPING?*

HONEY, THERE'S SOMETHING WE HAVE TO TALK ABOUT.

TEN MINUTES HE'S BEEN THERE ...

... NOW HE'S MOVING. GOOD.

ALFRED-- HOW DID YOU LIKE MY *PERFORMANCE?*

POSITIVELY *VAUDEVILLIAN,* SIR. I GATHER THE *REMAINING* BOTTLE OF *CLUB SODA* MAY BE LEFT IN ITS *PROPER* CONTAINER?

HMF. I SUPPOSE YOU'LL TAKE UP *FLYING* NEXT--

--LIKE THAT FELLOW IN *METROPOLIS.*

SKEEVERS TOLD US *WHERE,* *WHEN,* AND *HOW MUCH* MONEY YOU RECEIVED, FLASS.

AND YOU'VE BEEN SPENDING A LOT MORE THAN YOU'RE EARNING...

October 2

YOU'RE FACING *TEN YEARS* IN *PRISON,* FLASS.

THAT'S IF SKEEVERS IS ALIVE ENOUGH TO *TESTIFY.*

MY *CLIENT* DIDN'T *MEAN* THAT ...

October 5

YES, SIR. I KNOW ABOUT SGT. ESSEN. PLEASE DON'T BOTHER ME AGAIN.

October 7

Somebody slips rat poison into Skeevers' food.

Merkel gets his stomach pumped in time.

October 10

SKEEVERS IS STILL GOING TO TESTIFY AGAINST FLASS. DOESN'T CARE THAT HIS ATTORNEY QUIT.

WHATEVER HE'S SCARED OF, IT'S-- WHAT'S SO FUNNY, DENT?

October 12

LIEUTENANT GORDON?

IT'S A BOY. YOUR WIFE IS FINE.

...FOURTH IN A DARING SERIES OF CAT BURGLARIES. COMMISSIONER LOEB'S PRIVATE COLLECTION OF POP MEMORABILIA IS VALUED AT FORTY THOUSAND DOLLARS...

November 2

FORTY THOUSAND. SURE. SO WHERE AM I SUPPOSED TO *SELL* IT?

THOUGHT HE'D HAVE *JEWELS*--OR *PAINTINGS*--

--NOT *NOW*, OTTO...

THIS ONE DOESN'T EVEN *WORK.*

...LOEB WAS QUICK TO CHARGE THE *BATMAN* WITH THE CRIME...

MROWWRR

RIPP

BATMAN. THEY'RE GIVING THE CREDIT TO *BATMAN.* ACES.

SELINA--YOU DON'T WANT THEM TO KNOW IT WAS *YOU*...

...LEAVING GOTHAM TO *WONDER* --IS THE BATMAN A *VIGILANTE*--A *THIEF*--A *ROBIN HOOD*?--

-- IN OTHER NEWS, DETECTIVE *ARNOLD FLASS* FACES *INDICTMENT* TO-MORROW ON THOSE DRUG CHARGES...

I HEAR THE *ROMAN'S* GOT A *FORTUNE* IN OLD STUFF. MAYBE I'LL GIVE HIM A *SCRATCH* OR TWO BEFORE I *STEAL* IT. WON'T THINK IT'S *BATMAN* IF I GIVE HIM A *SCRATCH.*

WHERE'D I PUT THAT DAMN *COSTUME*...

≥Klik≤ AND I WANT TO BE A FRIEND TO YOU...

I *FIXED* IT, SELINA--

...COME ALONG NOW AND JOIN THE PARTY...

SELINA-- I *FIXED* IT--

SCRATCH HIM. ON THE *FACE.* JUST *ONCE.* HE COULD USE IT.

...INDUSTRY EXPERTS WERE *STUNNED* BY THE DEMONSTRATION OF *UNHEARD*-OF POSSIBILITIES FOR LIGHTWEIGHT, DURABLE *PLASTICS*...

WAYNE CHEMICALS

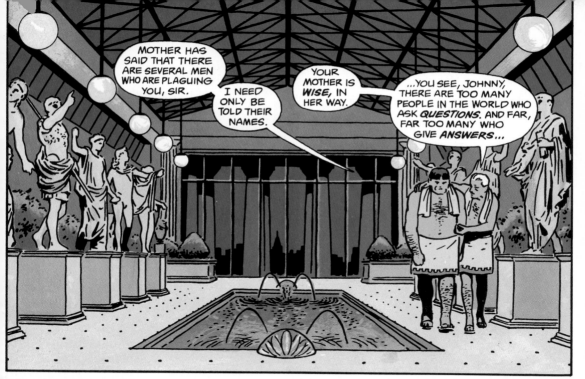

MY *FACE*--

--MY *FACE*--

November 3

MASTER *BRUCE*--I'VE JUST COME ACROSS A *FASCINATING* PIECE IN THE *TIMES*.

CONCERNS THE *EFFECTS* OF *SLEEP* AMONG THE MARGINALLY *SANE*...

QUIET, ALFRED.

...YOUR MOTHER IS *WISE,* IN HER WAY...

IF ONLY THAT *WOMAN* HADN'T BEEN THERE... THE ROMAN WAS ABOUT TO TELL HIS NEPHEW...

.."MARKED INCREASE IN PARANOIA" ,,, hmm ...

...*WHAPP* WE MUST AVOID MORE BAD *PUBLICITY,* JOHNNY...

I SHOULD'VE *CRIPPLED* THE ROMAN'S *NEPHEW.* WOULD'VE BOUGHT US *TIME.*

NO... HE'D HAVE JUST GOTTEN SOMEBODY *ELSE.* AT LEAST I KNOW WHO HE'S *USING.*

BATMAN ROBS BANK, SLASHES FACE!

≥WHRR≤... AVOID MORE BAD PUBLICITY... ≥KLIK≤

..."TENDENCY TOWARD ABERRANT, EVEN VIOLENT BEHAVIOR"...

HE DOESN'T WANT BAD PUBLICITY. IT FOLLOWS THAT HE WON'T *MURDER* ANYONE...

...THAT LEAVES *BLACKMAIL,* OR...

OFF AGAIN, SIR? SHALL I FETCH YOUR *TIGHTS?*

NEVER DURING THE *DAY,* ALFRED.

...LAST NIGHT'S INCIDENT CONNECTS THE *BATMAN* WITH THE RECENT *CAT BURGLARIES.* A WOMAN WITH *CLAWS*--PRESUMABLY BATMAN'S *ASSISTANT*-- IS SAID TO HAVE...

ASSISTANT. NOW I'M HIS *ASSISTANT.*

I'LL HAVE TO DO SOMETHING *REALLY* NASTY, NEXT TIME...

CAT FOOD

GORDON, JOHNNY. ONCE A MAN BECOMES A *FATHER* HE IS NEVER TRULY *FREE.*

LISTEN CLOSELY...

WAAAAHHH

FEEDING TIME.

MY TURN, HONEY...

WAAHHKWAHHH

EASY, NOW. GETTING IT WARM--

RINGG

WAAAAAAHHH

...YES, COMMISSIONER...

...SIR, MERKEL'S ON DUTY. HE CAN--

...YES, SIR. ON MY WAY.

GORDON IS LEAVING HIS APARTMENT. TELL THE ROMAN.

Third-rate witness in a nickel-and-dime open-and-shut domestic grievance and Loeb knows I've only had two hours sleep--

Maniac--

--should arrest the--

--wait a minute...

SCREEECHH

JIM--

If I let them go, they're dead--

KBLAMM

--can't go for a wound--

BLAMM

--Good, Barbara --stay low--

NNGG

BLAMM

--caught one in the shoulder--

--throws my aim off-- just for a second--

BLAMM

WASN'T SUPPOSED TO HAPPEN--

GET OUT OF HERE--HE'S CRAZY--

KPWEE

SKREEEE

Behind me a motorcycle starts--

BLAMM

GET *OUT* OF HERE, BARBARA--CALL A *COP*--

There--I can still see them--

--James--

DON'T-- I'LL *KILL* YOU--

MRS. GORDON. YOU HAVE TO TRUST ME.

I WON'T LET YOUR BOY DIE.

BLAMM

POWW

The driver hits the brakes, too late--going too fast--

--the bridge shakes--

--I listen to the rending metal and clattering glass--

--I listen--the radiator hisses, spits water on the street--

--I don't hear a human sound--

--I don't hear my baby cry--

93

--the metal rail digs into my back--

--he's heavy--

NO.

NO

WWAAAAHHHH

WAAAAAAHHHHH

WAAAHHHHGLBB

THAT'S RIGHT. GOOD BOY. SETTLE DOWN, NOW. YOU'RE SAFE.

YOU MUST BE WEARING SOME *ARMOR* UNDER THAT JACKET.

YES.

YOU KNOW, I'M PRACTICALLY *BLIND* WITHOUT MY GLASSES.

SIRENS COMING. YOU'D BETTER GO.

Turns out Flass is smarter than anybody knew.

He took notes on every little talk he'd had with Commissioner Loeb. Dates, times -- it was all there.

Two weeks and five days in jail and he remembered where he kept the notes.

Loeb's holding up pretty well under the strain.

Judge Norton's on the case, so I don't think Dent has a chance of putting him behind bars--

--but word is Loeb's conferring with the mayor on the terms of his resignation.

They've already got Grogan primed to replace him, who's worse. Still, things aren't so bad, right now.

The Roman's been at war with his sister ever since he tried to get a hired knife slid between his nephew's ribs.

I had a few run-ins with his sister, back in Chicago, a few years ago. I don't envy the Roman.

December 3

They were all too busy to stand in the way of my promotion to Captain.

Sarah's in New York, doing well, I hear.

Barbara's not crazy about the marriage counselor, but we're making progress.

As for me -- well, there's a real panic on. Somebody's threatened to poison the Gotham reservoir.

Calls himself the Joker.

I've got a friend coming who might be able to help.

Should be here any minute.

FRANK MILLER

is the writer of *Ronin, Batman: The Dark Knight Returns*, and
Elektra: Assassin. He is now working on three new graphic
novels: *Elektra Lives Again*, with Lynn Varley; *Give Me Liberty*,
with Dave Gibbons; and *Hard Boiled*, with Geof Darrow. Miller
lives in Los Angeles and loves writing crime stories.

DAVID MAZZUCCHELLI

drew his first professional comic book while majoring in painting
at the Rhode Island School of Design. After a handful of jobs for
Marvel and DC Comics, he became the regular artist on Marvel's
Daredevil, where he first collaborated with writer Frank Miller to
produce the highly successful and critically acclaimed seven-part
story "Born Again." His work on *Batman* and *Daredevil* has
earned him both an American Comic Book Award and Spain's
Haxtur Prize.

RICHMOND LEWIS

received her B.F.A. in painting from the Rhode Island School of
Design and afterwards lived and painted in Europe for nine
months. Richmond has exhibited her paintings and drawings,
and she recently had a one-person show in New York City.